HURRICANE CITY

BY **Sarah Weeks** • ILLUSTRATIONS BY **James Warhola**

A Laura Geringer Book
An Imprint of HarperCollinsPublishers

Welcome to HURRICANE CITY, friends,

Where hurricane season never ends.

We get them big,

We get them small—

Sooner or later we get them all. . . .

**Hurricane ALVIN swept through town
And turned the flowers upside down.**

**B** Hurricane **BERTHA** blew about
And turned umbrellas inside out.

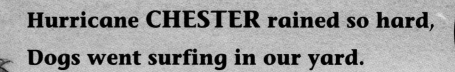

Hurricane CHESTER rained so hard,
Dogs went surfing in our yard.

C

**D**Hurricane **DINAH** snapped a wire—
We squirted hoses at the fire.

Hurricane **ETHAN** came and went
And left the mailbox slightly bent.

E

F

Hurricane **FRANCES** made us laugh,
She cut the beauty shop in half.

Hurricane **GABRIEL** blew like mad—
Father lost what hair he had.

G

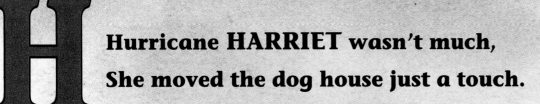

Hurricane **HARRIET** wasn't much,
She moved the dog house just a touch.

Hurricane IGOR caused the flood
That filled the swimming pool with mud.

I

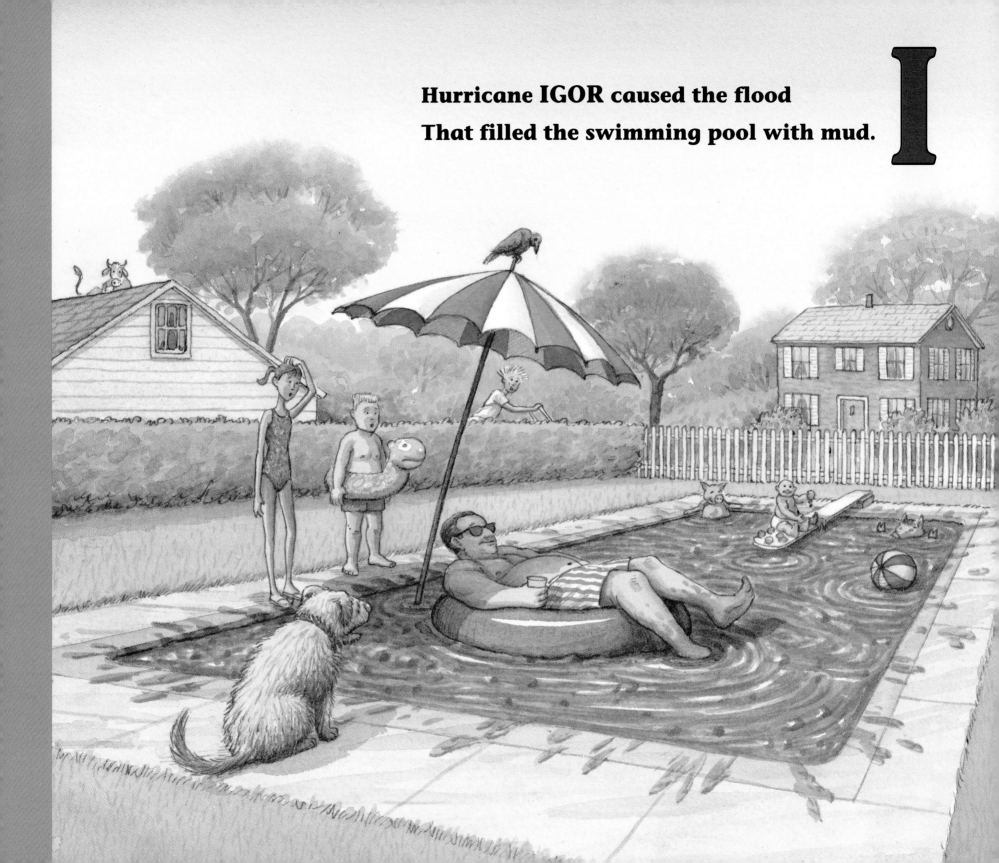

J Hurricane JANE was short but sweet,
We floated picnics down the street.

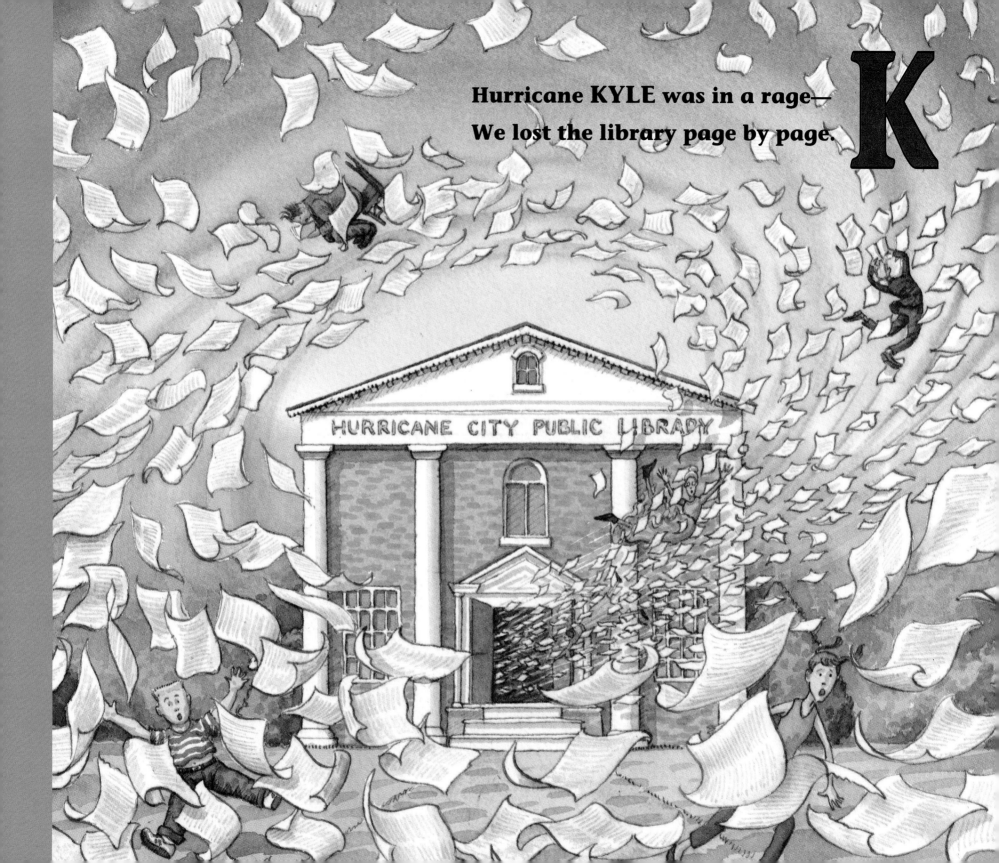

Hurricane KYLE was in a rage—
We lost the library page by page.

K

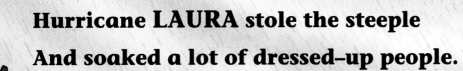

L Hurricane LAURA stole the steeple
And soaked a lot of dressed–up people.

Hurricane **MIKE** made hailstones fall—
In half an hour we sold them all.

M

FRESH HAILSTONES

Hurricane City's Finest!

N

Hurricane NATTY blew all night—
By morning nothing looked quite right.

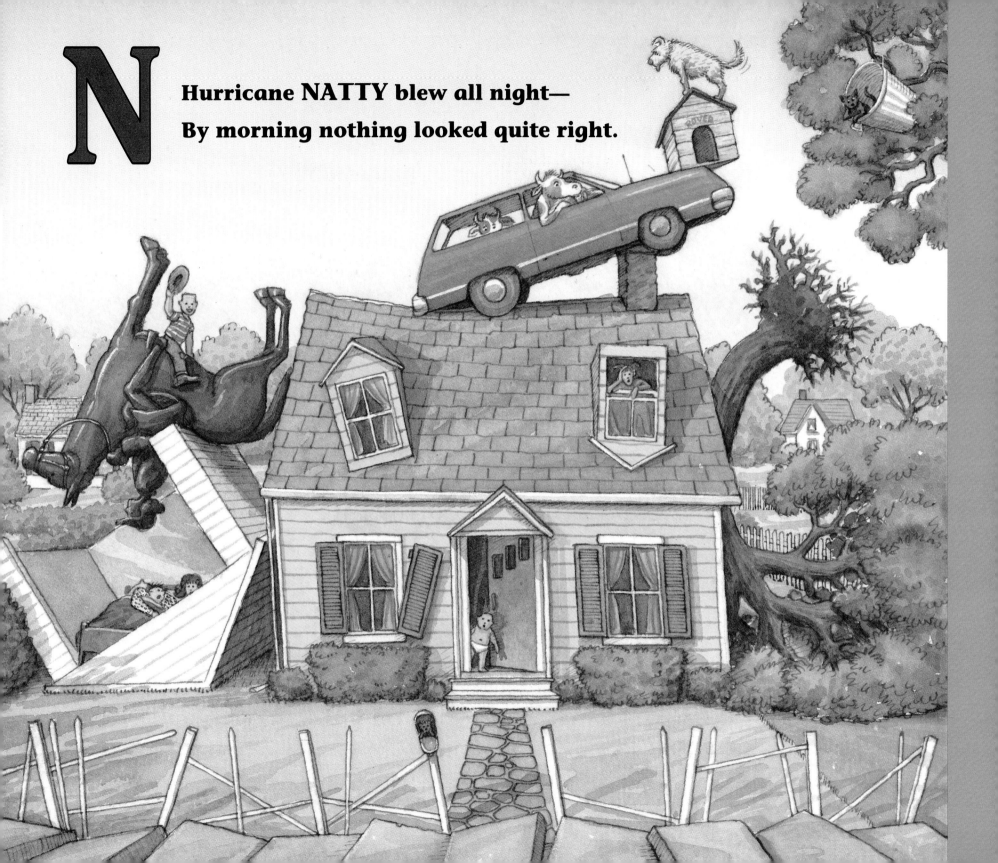

Hurricane OPAL huffed and puffed,
Sandwiches came all unstuffed.

O

P Hurricane PETE rained cats and dogs
And cows and geese and fish and frogs.

Hurricane QUINCY—he was weird,
The next-door neighbors disappeared.

Q

R Hurricane **ROBERT** hit the roof
And blew right down the chimney—poof!

Hurricane SAL, now she was cruel,
Because of her they canceled school.

S

**T**Hurricane TOMMY stepped right in
And helped the hometown team to win.

Hurricane URSULA hurried by
And hung the clothesline way up high.

U

V

Hurricane VICTOR caused a stir
By blowing off a lot of fur.

Hurricane WENDY stayed a week—
She tore off Chicken Lickin's beak.

W

Hurricane **XERXES** was just hot air—
We barely noticed he was there.

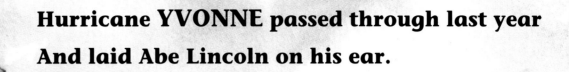

Hurricane **YVONNE** passed through last year
And laid Abe Lincoln on his ear.

Y

ABE
LINCOLN

Hurricane ZACK is coming this way—

He'll be here very soon I'd say. . . .

We get them big,

We get them small—

Sooner or later we get them all.

For Michael

— S.W.

**For Marion and Howard
of Barnegat Light**

— J.W.

HURRICANE CITY
Text copyright © 1993 by Sarah Weeks
Illustrations copyright © 1993 by James Warhola
Printed in the U.S.A. All rights reserved.
Designed by David Saylor

1 2 3 4 5 6 7 8 9 10
❖
First Edition

Library of Congress Cataloging-in-Publication Data   Weeks, Sarah.   Hurricane City / by Sarah Weeks ; illustrations by James Warhola.   p. cm.
"A Laura Geringer book."   Summary: A family describes in humorous rhyme the impact of hurricanes, from Alvin through Zack, on their city
where hurricane season never ends.   ISBN 0-06-021572-0. — ISBN 0-06-021573-9 (lib. bdg.)   [1. Alphabet.   2. Hurricanes—Fiction.   3. Stories in rhyme.]
I. Warhola, James, ill.   II. Title.   PZ8.3.W4125Hu   1993   92-23389   [E]—dc20   CIP   AC